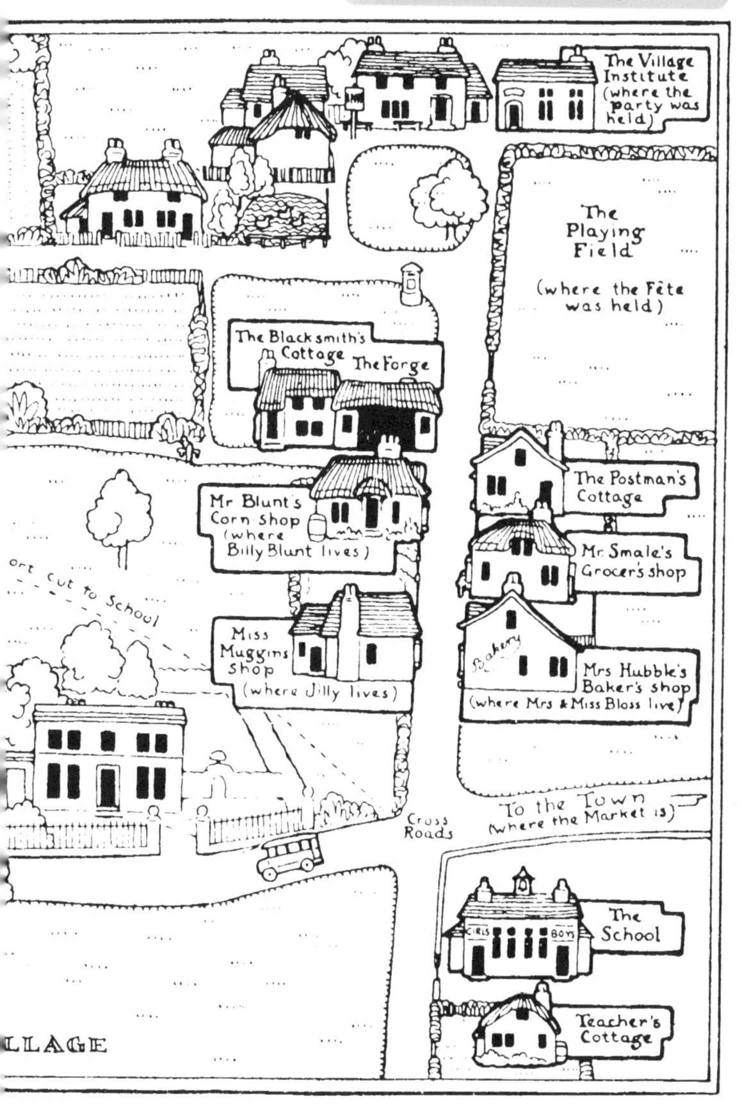
INN
The Village Institute (where the party was held)
The Playing Field
(where the Fête was held)
The Blacksmith's Cottage
The Forge
The Postman's Cottage
Mr Blunt's Corn shop (where Billy Blunt lives)
Mr Smale's Grocer's shop
ort cut to School
Miss Muggins Shop
(where Jilly lives)
Bakery
Mrs Hubble's Baker's shop
(where Mrs & Miss Bloss live)
Cross Roads
To the Town (where the Market is)
GIRLS
BOYS
The School
Teacher's Cottage
LLAGE

MILLY-MOLLY-MANDY'S Adventures

Other Milly-Molly-Mandy books

Family

Friends

School Days

Joyce Lankester Brisley

MILLY-MOLLY-MANDY'S Adventures

MACMILLAN CHILDREN'S BOOKS

First published by Kingfisher 2005

This edition published 2012 by Macmillan Children's Books
a division of Macmillan Publishers Limited
20 New Wharf Road, London N1 9RR
Basingstoke and Oxford
Associated companies throughout the world
www.panmacmillan.com

ISBN 978-0-230-75500-0

The stories in this collection first appeared in
More of Milly-Molly-Mandy (1929)
Further Doings of Milly-Molly-Mandy (1932)
Milly-Molly-Mandy and Billy Blunt (1967)
published by George G. Harrap & Co. Ltd

1 3 5 7 9 8 6 4 2

A CIP catalogue record for this book is available from the British Library.

Printed and bound in China

Publisher's Note

*The stories in this collection are reproduced in the form in which they appeared
upon first publication in the UK by George G. Harrap & Co. Ltd.
All spellings remain consistent with these original editions.*

Contents

The Nice White Cottage with the Thatched Roof (where Milly-Molly-Mandy lives)
Brook
The Meadow (where M-M-M and Billy Blunt practised racing)
The Barn (where M-M-M gave a party)
The Moggs's Cottage (where little-friend-Susan lives)
Short cut to School (only used in dry weather)
Woods
To Another Village
MAP of th

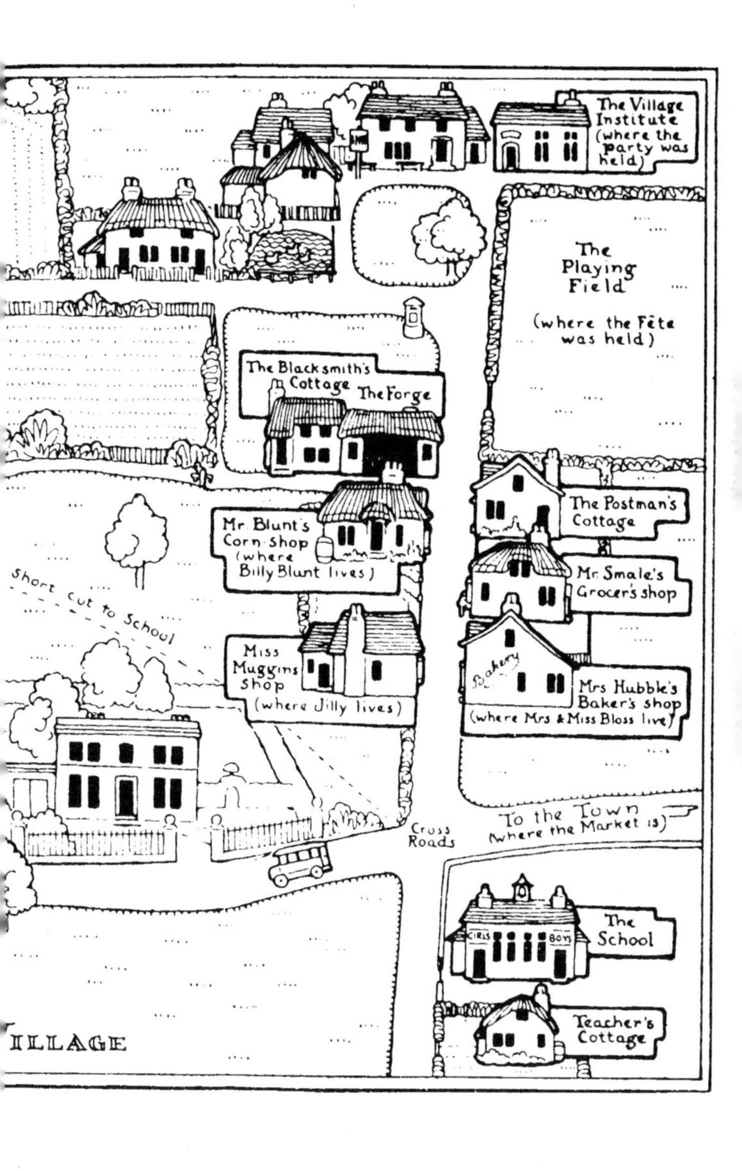
The Village Institute (where the party was held)
The Playing Field (where the Fête was held)
The Blacksmith's Cottage
The Forge
Mr. Blunt's Corn Shop (where Billy Blunt lives)
The Postman's Cottage
Mr. Smale's Grocer's shop
Short cut to School
Miss Muggins Shop (where Jilly lives)
Bakery
Mrs Hubble's Baker's shop (where Mrs. & Miss Bloss live)
Cross Roads
To the Town (where the Market is)
GIRLS
BOYS
The School
Teacher's Cottage
ILLAGE

Milly-Molly-Mandy Has an Adventure

Once upon a time, one Saturday afternoon, Milly-Molly-Mandy had quite an adventure.

There was a special children's film showing at the cinema in the next village, and Milly-Molly-Mandy and little-friend-Susan were going to it, by bus, quite by themselves!

"Keep together, and don't talk to strangers," said Mother, giving Milly-Molly-Mandy the money for the cinema and for the bus, there and back.

"But supposing strangers speak to us?"

said Milly-Molly-Mandy.

"Always answer politely," said Mother, "but no more than that."

So Milly-Molly-Mandy set off from the nice white cottage with the thatched roof, down the road with the hedges each side to the Moggses' cottage where little-friend-Susan was waiting for her. And they walked on together to the cross-roads, feeling very important, to catch the bus.

There was plenty of time, but they thought they had better run the last part of the way, to be on the safe side. But nobody was waiting at the cross-roads, so they wondered if they had missed the bus after all.

Then one or two people came up and waited, so it couldn't have gone. And presently it came in sight.

And just as everybody was getting on who do you suppose came along and got on too? – Why, Billy Blunt!

Milly-Molly-Mandy and little-friend-Susan took their seats and paid their half-fares, and pocketed the change carefully (three pennies for Milly-Molly-Mandy, a threepenny piece for little-friend-Susan). And then they sat looking out of the windows to make sure they didn't get carried past the cinema.

Billy Blunt had made for a seat right in front, looking as if he were quite used to doing this sort of thing himself. (But he couldn't have been, really!) He managed to be first to get off the moment the bus stopped, so they didn't actually see if he went into the cinema.

Inside, it was so dark you couldn't recognize anybody. Milly-Molly-Mandy and little-friend-Susan held hands tight, not to lose one another.

It was all very exciting.

And so was the film. They wished it needn't end. When it was all over it seemed funny to come out into the daylight again and find the same ordinary world outside.

They saw Billy Blunt coming away, talking with another boy. So they walked straight to the bus stop and began waiting. (The bus ran every hour, and if one had just gone they might be a long time getting home.)

Suddenly little-friend-Susan said loudly, "My money!" and began rummaging in her coat-pocket.

Milly-Molly-Mandy said, "Why? Where?" and began rummaging in her own. (But her three pennies were safe all right).

"My threepenny piece!" said little-friend-Susan; "I had it here. . ."

She looked in her right-hand pocket, then in her left, then in her hands. Then Milly-Molly-Mandy looked.

Then they looked on the pavement, and in the gutter.

"You must have dropped it in the cinema, Susan," said Milly-Molly-Mandy. "Let's go back and ask."

"But I didn't," said little-friend-Susan. "I felt it in my pocket as we came out."

So they looked all along the pavement. But still they couldn't find it.

"Well, we've just got to walk home," said Milly-Molly-Mandy, at last. "You can't go by yourself. We'll have to walk together."

"It's too far to walk," said little-friend-Susan, nearly crying. Just then Billy Blunt came up to join the queue. Milly-Molly-Mandy said to him, "She's lost her money!"

Billy Blunt did not know what to say, so he said nothing.

A gypsy woman standing near with a baby and a big basket said, "There now! Lost your money, have you, ducks?"

Milly-Molly-Mandy said again, "We've got to walk home."

Billy Blunt said, "It's too far." Then he said, "Here, have mine. I'll manage."

But Milly-Molly-Mandy and little-friend-Susan said together, "You can't walk that far by yourself!"

The gypsy woman began fumbling under her apron for her purse.

"I may have just a spare copper or two," she said. "Where does the little lady live? I'll call on her ma, and she can pay me back some day!"

Milly-Molly-Mandy, remembering what

"She's lost her money!"

Mother said, answered politely, "No, thank you very much!" – when at that moment the bus came in sight.

"Here!" said Billy Blunt, holding out his money.

Milly-Molly-Mandy and little-friend-Susan didn't like to take it. They couldn't think what to do.

An old truck laden with empty cans and things was coming rattling down the road. It overtook the bus and was clattering past the bus-stop when Milly-Molly-Mandy suddenly started waving her arms wildly at it.

"Cyril, stop! Cyril!" she shouted.

The truck slowed down,

and a tousled head looked back from the driver's seat.

"It's Cyril!" Milly-Molly-Mandy told the others, excitedly. "He drives things to the station for Uncle sometimes!" She ran forward. "Oh, Cyril! May I ride home with you?" she asked.

"You may not," said Cyril. "In that get-up? – I'd have your ma after me. Anyhow, I'm not going by your house today – only to the cross-roads."

Little-friend-Susan pulled at Milly-Molly-Mandy's sleeve.

"But Milly-Molly-Mandy! You know we've got to keep together!"

The bus was drawing up. People were beginning to get on.

Billy Blunt asked Cyril quickly, "Can you take me?"

"If you want," said Cyril. "But hop on quick."

The bus was tooting for him to get out of the way.

Billy Blunt pushed his money at little-friend-Susan, saying, "Go on – hurry!" Then he clambered into the truck beside Cyril, helped by Cyril's very grubby hand, and off they went rattling down the road.

"Now then, you two!" the bus-driver called out of his small side window, "are you coming with us or aren't you? We haven't got all day, you know."

And Milly-Molly-Mandy and little-friend-Susan (full of smiles) rushed to scramble on to the bus. And off they went, after the truck, down the road, and along the winding leafy lanes.

Billy Blunt was waiting at the cross-roads to see them arrive. He looked quite pleased with himself! (He had an oily smear down one leg and his hands were black.)

"I got here quicker than you did," was all he said, when they thanked him.

And – do you know! – that threepenny piece of little-friend-Susan's was found after all!

It had worked through the small hole in her coat-pocket down into the lining. And she was able to work it out again and pay Billy Blunt back the next day.

Milly-Molly-Mandy Camps Out

Once upon a time Milly-Molly-Mandy and Toby the dog went down to the village, to Miss Muggins's shop, on an errand for Mother; and as they passed Mr Blunt's corn-shop Milly-Molly-Mandy saw something new in the little garden at the side. It looked like a small, shabby sort of tent, with a slit in the top and a big checked patch sewn on the side.

Milly-Molly-Mandy wondered what it was doing there. But she didn't see Billy Blunt anywhere about, so she couldn't ask him.

When she came out of Miss Muggins's shop she had another good look over the palings into the Blunts's garden. And while she was looking Billy Blunt came out of their house door with some old rugs and a pillow in his arms.

"Hullo, Billy!" said Milly-Molly-Mandy. "What's that tent-thing?"

"It's a tent," said Billy Blunt, not liking its being called a "thing".

"But what's it for?" asked Milly-Molly-Mandy.

"It's mine," said Billy Blunt.

"Yours? Your very own? Is it?" said Milly-Molly-Mandy. "Ooh, do let me come and look at it!"

"You can if you want to," said Billy Blunt. "I'm going to sleep in it tonight – camp out."

Milly-Molly-Mandy was very interested indeed. She looked at it well, outside and in. She could only just stand up in it. Billy Blunt had spread an old mackintosh for a ground sheet, and there was a box in one corner to hold a bottle of water and a mug, and his electric torch, and such necessary things; and when the front flap of the tent was closed you couldn't see anything outside, except a tiny bit of sky and some green leaves through the tear in the top.

Milly-Molly-Mandy didn't want to come out a bit, but Billy Blunt wanted to put his bedding in.

"Isn't it beautiful! Where did you get it, Billy?" she asked.

"My cousin gave it to me," said Billy Blunt. "Used it when he went on cycling holidays. He's got a new one now. I put that patch on, myself."

Milly-Molly-Mandy thought she could have done it better; but still it was quite good for a boy, so she duly admired it, and offered to mend the other place. But Billy Blunt didn't think it was worth it, as it would only tear away again – and he liked a bit of air, anyhow.

"Shan't you feel funny out here all by yourself when everybody else is asleep?" said Milly-Molly-Mandy. "Oh, I wish I had a tent too!" Then she said goodbye, and ran with Toby the dog back home to the nice white cottage with the thatched roof, thinking of the tent all the way.

She didn't see little-friend-Susan as

she passed the Moggses' cottage along the road; but when she got as far as the meadow she saw her swinging her baby sister on the big gate.

"Hullo, Milly-Molly-Mandy! I was just looking for you," said little-friend-Susan, lifting Baby Moggs down. And Milly-Molly-Mandy told her all about Billy Blunt's new tent, and how he was going to sleep out, and how she wished she had a tent too.

Little-friend-Susan was almost as interested as Milly-Molly-Mandy. "Can't we make a tent and play in it in your meadow?" she said. "It would be awful fun!"

So they got some bean poles and bits of sacking from the barn and dragged them down into the meadow. And they had great fun that day trying to make a tent; only they couldn't get it to stay up properly.

Next morning little-friend-Susan came to play "tents" in the meadow again. And this time they tried with an old counterpane, which Mother had given them, and two kitchen chairs; and they managed to rig up quite a good tent by laying the poles across the chair-backs and draping the counterpane over. They fastened down the spread-out sides with stones; and the ends, where the chairs were, they hung with sacks. And there they had a perfectly good tent, really quite big enough for two – so long as the two were small, and didn't mind being a bit crowded!

They were just sitting in it, eating apples and pretending they had no other home to live in, when they heard a "*Hi*" -ing from the gate; and when they peeped out there was Billy Blunt, with a great bundle in his arms, trying to get the gate open. So they ran across the grass and opened it for him.

"What have you got? Is it your tent? Did you sleep out last night?" asked Milly-Molly-Mandy

"Look here," said Billy Blunt, "do you think your father would mind, supposing I pitched my tent in your field? My folk don't like it in our garden – say it looks too untidy."

Milly-Molly-Mandy was quite sure Father wouldn't mind. So Billy Blunt put the bundle down inside the gate and went off to ask (for of course you never camp anywhere without saying "please" to the owner first). And Father didn't mind a bit, so long as no papers or other rubbish were left about.

So Billy Blunt set up his tent near the others', which was not too far from the nice white cottage with the thatched roof (because it's funny what a long way off from everybody you feel when you've got only a tent round you at night!). And then he went home to fetch his other goods; and Milly-Molly-Mandy and little-friend-Susan sat in his tent, and wished and wished that their mothers would let them sleep out in the meadow that night.

When Billy Blunt came back with his rugs and things (loaded up on his box on wheels) they asked him if it were a very creepy feeling to sleep out of doors.

And Billy Blunt (having slept out once)

said, "Oh, you soon get used to it," and asked why they didn't try it in their tent.

So then Milly-Molly-Mandy and little-friend-Susan looked at each other, and said firmly, "Let's ask!" So little-friend-Susan went with Milly-Molly-Mandy up to the nice white cottage with the thatched roof, where Mother was just putting a treacle-tart into the oven.

She looked very doubtful when Milly-Molly-Mandy told her what they wanted to do. Then she shut the oven door, and wiped her hands, and said, well, she would just come and look at the tent they had made first. And when she had looked and considered, she said, well, if it were still very fine and dry by the evening perhaps Milly-Molly-Mandy might sleep out there, just for once. And Mother found a rubber ground-sheet and some old blankets and cushions, and gave them to her.

Then Milly-Molly-Mandy went with little-friend-Susan to the Moggses' cottage, where Mrs Moggs was just putting their potatoes on to boil.

She looked very doubtful at first; and

then she said, well, if Milly-Molly-Mandy's mother had been out to see, and thought it was all right, and if it were a *very* nice, fine evening, perhaps little-friend-Susan might sleep out, just for once.

So all the rest of the day the three

Then little-friend-Susan and Billy Blunt crawled out

were very busy, making preparations and watching the sky. And when they all went home for supper the evening was beautifully still and warm, without a single cloud.

So, after supper, they all met together again in the meadow, in the sunset. And they shut and tied up the meadow gate. (It was all terribly exciting!)

And Mother came out, with Father and Grandpa and Grandma and Uncle and Aunty, to see that all was right, and their ground-sheets well spread under their bedding.

Then Milly-Molly-Mandy and little-friend-Susan crawled into their tent, and Billy Blunt crawled into his tent. And presently Milly-Molly-Mandy crawled out again in her pyjamas, and ran about with bare feet on the grass with Toby the dog; and then little-friend-Susan and Billy Blunt, in their pyjamas, crawled out and ran about too (because it feels so very nice, and so sort of new, to be running about under the sky in your pyjamas!).

And Father and Mother and Grandpa and Grandma and Uncle and Aunty laughed, and looked on as if they wouldn't mind doing it too, if they weren't so grown up.

Then Mother said, "Now I think it's time you campers popped into bed. Goodnight!"

And they went off home.

So Milly-Molly-Mandy and little-friend-Susan called "Goodnight!" and crawled into one tent, and Billy Blunt caught Toby the dog and crawled into the other.

And the trees outside grew slowly blacker and blacker until they couldn't be seen at all; and the owls hooted; and a far-away cow mooed; and now and then Toby the dog wuffed, because he thought he heard a rabbit; and sometimes

Milly-Molly-Mandy or little-friend-Susan squeaked, because they thought they felt a spider walking on them. And once Billy Blunt called out to ask if they were still awake, and they said they were, and was he? and he said of course he was.

And then at last they all fell asleep.

And in no time at all the sun was shining through their tents, telling them to wake up and come out, because it was the next day.

And Billy Blunt and Milly-Molly-Mandy and little-friend-Susan DID enjoy that camping-out night!

Milly-Molly-Mandy Goes to the Sea

Once upon a time – what do you think? – Milly-Molly-Mandy was going to be taken to the seaside!

Milly-Molly-Mandy had never seen the sea in all her life before, and ever since Mother came back from her seaside holiday with her friend Mrs Hooker, and told Milly-Molly-Mandy about the splashy waves and the sand and the little crabs, Milly-Molly-Mandy had just longed to go there herself.

Father and Mother and Grandpa and Grandma and Uncle and Aunty just longed for her to go too, because they knew she would like it so much. But they were all so busy, and then, you know, holidays cost quite a lot of money.

So Milly-Molly-Mandy played 'seaside' instead, by the little brook in the meadow, with little-friend-Susan and Billy Blunt and the shells Mother had brought home for her. (And it was a very nice game indeed, but still Milly-Molly-Mandy did wish sometimes that it could be the real sea!)

Then one day little-friend-Susan went with her mother and baby sister to stay with a relation who let lodgings by the sea. And little-friend-Susan wrote Milly-Molly-Mandy a postcard saying how lovely it was, and how she did wish Milly-Molly-Mandy was there; and Mrs Moggs wrote Mother a postcard saying couldn't some of them manage to come down just for a day excursion, one Saturday?

Father and Mother and Grandpa and Grandma and Uncle and Aunty thought something really ought to be done about that, and they talked it over, while Milly-Molly-Mandy listened with all her ears.

But Father said he couldn't go, because he had to get his potatoes up; Mother said she couldn't go because it was baking day, and, besides, she had just had a lovely seaside holiday; Grandpa said he couldn't go, because it was market day; Grandma said she wasn't really very fond of train journeys; Uncle said he oughtn't to leave his cows and chickens.

But then they all said Aunty could quite well leave the sweeping and dusting for that one day.

So Aunty only said it seemed too bad that she should have all the fun. And then she and Milly-Molly-Mandy hugged each other, because it was so very exciting.

Milly-Molly-Mandy ran off to tell Billy Blunt at once, because she felt she would burst if she didn't tell someone. And Billy Blunt did wish he could be going too, but his father and mother were always busy.

Milly-Molly-Mandy told Aunty, and Aunty said, "Tell Billy Blunt to ask his mother to let him come with us, and I'll see after him!"

So Billy Blunt did, and Mrs Blunt said it was very kind of Aunty and she'd be glad to let him go.

Milly-Molly-Mandy hoppity-skipped like anything, because she was so very pleased; and Billy Blunt was very pleased too, though he didn't hoppity-skip, because he always thought he was too old for such doings (but he wasn't really!).

So now they were able to plan together for Saturday, which made it much more fun.

Mother had an old bathing-dress which she cut down to fit Milly-Molly-Mandy, and the bits over she made into a flower for the shoulder (and it looked a very smart bathing-dress indeed). Billy Blunt borrowed a swimming-suit from another boy at school (but it hadn't any flower on the shoulder, of course not!).

Then Billy Blunt said to Milly-Molly-Mandy, "If you've got swimming-suits you ought to swim. We'd better practise."

But Milly-Molly-Mandy said, "We haven't got enough water."

Billy Blunt said, "Practise in air, then – better than nothing."

So they fetched two old boxes from the barn out into the yard, and then lay on them (on their fronts) and spread out their arms

and kicked with their legs just as if they were swimming. And when Uncle came along to fetch a wheelbarrow he said it really made him feel quite cool to see them!

He showed them how to turn their hands properly, and kept calling out, "Steady! Steady! Not so fast!" as he watched them.

And then Uncle lay on his front on the box and showed them how (and he looked so funny!), and then they tried again, and Uncle said it was better that time.

So they practised until they were quite out of breath. And then they pretended to dive off the boxes, and they splashed and swallowed mouthfuls of air and swam races to the gate and shivered and dried themselves with old sacks – and it was almost as much fun as if it were real water!

Well, Saturday came at last, and Aunty

and Milly-Molly-Mandy met Billy Blunt at nine o'clock by the cross-roads. And then they went in the red bus to the station in the next town.

And then they went in the train, rumpty-te-tump, rumpty-te-tump, all the way down to the sea.

And you can't imagine how exciting it was, when they got out at last, to walk down a road knowing they would see the real sea at the bottom! Milly-Molly-Mandy got so excited that she didn't want to look till they were up quite close.

So Billy Blunt (who had seen it once before) pulled her along right on to the edge of the sand, and then he said suddenly, "Now look!"

And Milly-Molly-Mandy looked.

And there was the sea, all jumping with sparkles in the sunshine, as far as ever you could see. And little-friend-Susan,

with bare legs and frock tucked up, came tearing over the sand to meet them from where Mrs Moggs and Baby Moggs were sitting by a wooden breakwater.

Wasn't it fun!

They took off their shoes and their socks and their hats, and they wanted to take off their clothes and bathe, but Aunty said they must have dinner first. So they sat round and ate sandwiches and cake and fruit which Aunty had brought in a basket. And the Moggses had theirs too out of a basket.

Then they played in the sand with Baby Moggs (who liked having her legs buried), and paddled a bit and found crabs (they didn't take them away from the water, though).

And then Aunty and Mrs Moggs said they might bathe now if they wanted to. So (as it was a very quiet sort of beach) Milly-Molly-Mandy undressed behind Aunty, and little-friend-Susan undressed behind Mrs Moggs, and Billy Blunt undressed behind the breakwater.

And then they ran right into the water in their bathing-dresses. (And little-friend-Susan thought Milly-Molly-Mandy's bathing-dress was smart, with the flower on the shoulder!)

But, dear me! Water-swimming feels so different from land-swimming, and Milly-

Molly-Mandy couldn't manage at all well with the little waves splashing at her all the time. Billy Blunt swished about in the water with a very grim face, and looked exactly as if he were swimming; but when Milly-Molly-Mandy asked him, he said, "No! My arms swim, but my legs only walk!"

It was queer, for it had seemed quite easy in the barn-yard.

But they went on pretending and pretending to swim until Aunty called them out. And then they dried themselves with towels and got into their clothes again; and Billy Blunt said, well, anyhow, he supposed they were just that much nearer swimming properly than they were before; and Milly-Molly-Mandy said she supposed next time they might p'r'aps be able to lift their feet off the ground for a minute at any rate; and little-friend-Susan

They ran right into the water in their bathing dresses

said she was sure she had swallowed a shrimp! (But that was only her fun!)

Then they played and explored among the rock-pools and had tea on the sand. And after tea Mrs Moggs and Baby Moggs and little-friend-Susan walked with them back to the station; and Aunty and Milly-Molly-Mandy and Billy Blunt went in the train, rumpty-te-tump, rumpty-te-tump, all the way home again.

And Milly-Molly-Mandy was so sleepy when she got to the nice white cottage with the thatched roof that she had only just time to kiss Father and Mother and Grandpa and Grandma and Uncle and Aunty goodnight and get into bed before she fell fast asleep.

Milly-Molly-Mandy Goes on an Expedition

Once upon a time it was a Monday-bank-holiday. Milly-Molly-Mandy had been looking forward to this Monday-bank-holiday for a long time, more than a week, for she and Billy Blunt had been planning to go for a long fishing expedition on that day.

It was rather exciting.

They were to get up very early, and take their dinners with them, and their rods and lines and jam-jars, and go off all on their own along by the brook, and not be back until quite late in the day.

Milly-Molly-Mandy went to bed the night before with all the things she wanted for the expedition arranged beside her bed – a new little tin mug (to drink out of), and a bottle (for drinking water), and a large packet of bread-and-butter and an egg and a banana (for her dinner), and a jam-jar (to carry the fish in), and a little green fishing net (to catch them with), and some string and a safety-pin (which it is always useful to have), and her school satchel (to put things in). For when you are going off for the whole day you want quite a lot of things with you.

When Milly-Molly-Mandy woke up on Monday-bank-holiday morning she thought to herself, "Oh, dear! It is a grey sort of day – I do hope it isn't going to rain!"

But anyhow she knew she was going to enjoy herself, and she jumped up and washed and dressed and put on her hat and the satchel strap over her shoulder.

And then the sunshine came creeping over the trees outside, and Milly-Molly-Mandy saw that it had only been a grey day because she was up before the sun – and she felt a sort of little skip inside, because she was so very sure she was going to enjoy herself!

Just then there came a funny gritty sound like a handful of earth on the window pane, and when she put her head out there was Billy Blunt, eating a large piece of bread-and-butter and grinning up at her, looking very businesslike with rod and line and jam-jar and bulging satchel.

Milly-Molly-Mandy called out of the window in a loud whisper, "Isn't it a lovely day? I'm just coming!"

And Billy Blunt called back in a loud whisper, "Come on! Hurry up! It's getting late."

So Milly-Molly-Mandy hurried up like anything, and picked up her things and ran creeping downstairs, past Father's and Mother's room, and Grandpa's and Grandma's room, and Uncle's and Aunty's room. And she filled her bottle at the tap in the scullery, and took up the thick slice of bread-and-butter which Mother had left between two plates ready for her breakfast, and unlocked the back door and slipped out into the fresh morning air.

And there they were, off on their Monday-bank-holiday expedition!

"Isn't it lovely!" said Milly-Molly-Mandy, with a little hop.

"Umm! Come on!" said Billy Blunt.

So they went out of the back gate and across the meadow to the brook, walking very businesslikely and enjoying their bread-and-butter very thoroughly.

"We'll go that way," said Billy Blunt, "because that's the way we don't generally go."

"And when we come to a nice place we'll fish," said Milly-Molly-Mandy.

"But that won't be for a long way yet," said Billy Blunt.

So they went on walking very businesslikely (they had eaten their bread-and-butter by this time) until they had left the nice white cottage with the thatched roof a long way behind, and the sun was shining down quite hotly.

"It seems like a real expedition when you have the whole day to do it in, doesn't it?" said Milly-Molly-Mandy. "I wonder what the time is now!"

"Not time for dinner yet," said Billy Blunt. "But I could eat it."

"So could I," said Milly-Molly-Mandy. "Let's have a drink of water." So they each had a little tin mug full of water, and drank it very preciously to make it last, as the bottle didn't hold much.

The brook was too muddy and weedy for drinking, but it was a very interesting brook.One place, where it had got rather blocked up, was just full of tadpoles – they caught ever so many with their hands and put them in the jam-jars, and watched them swim about and wiggle their little black tails and open and shut their

Off on their Monday bank-holiday expedition

little black mouths. Then farther on were lots of stepping-stones in the stream, and Milly-Molly-Mandy and Billy Blunt had a fine time scrambling about from one to another.

Billy Blunt slipped once, with one foot into the water, so he took off his boots and socks and tied them round his neck. And it looked so nice that Milly-Molly-Mandy took off one boot and sock and tried it too. But the water and the stones were so-o cold that she put them on again, and just tried to be fairly careful how she went. But even so she slipped once, and caught her frock on a branch and pulled the button off, and had to fasten it together with a safety-pin. (So wasn't it a good thing she had brought one with her?)

Presently they came to a big flat mossy stone beside the brook. And Milly-Molly-Mandy said, "That's where we ought to eat our dinners, isn't it? I wonder what the time is now!"

Billy Blunt looked round and considered; and then he said, "Somewhere about noon, I should say. Might think about eating soon, as we had breakfast early. Less to carry, too."

And Milly-Molly-Mandy said, "Let's spread it out all ready, anyhow! It's a lovely place here."

So they laid the food out on the flat stone, with the bottle of water and little tin mug in the middle, and it looked so good and they felt so hungry that, of course, they just had to set to and eat it all up straight away.

And it did taste nice!

And the little black tadpoles in the glass jam-jars beside them swam round and round, and wiggled their little black tails and opened and shut their little black mouths; till at last Milly-Molly-Mandy said, "We've taken them away from their dinners, haven't we? Let's put them back now."

And Billy Blunt said, "Yes. We'll want the pots for real fishes soon."

So they emptied the tadpoles back into the brook where they wiggled away at once to their meals.

"Look! There's a fish!" cried Milly-Molly-Mandy, pointing. And Billy Blunt hurried and fetched his rod and line, and settled to fishing in real earnest.

Milly-Molly-Mandy went a little farther down-stream, and poked about with her net in the water; and soon she caught a fish, and put it in her jam-jar, and ran to show it to Billy Blunt. And Billy Blunt said, "Huh!" But he said it wasn't proper fishing without a rod and line, so it didn't really count.

But Milly-Molly-Mandy liked it quite well that way, all the same.

So they fished and they fished along the banks and sometimes they saw quite big fish, two or three inches long, and Billy Blunt got quite excited and borrowed Milly-Molly-Mandy's net; and they got a number of fish in their jam-jars.

"Oh, don't you wish we'd brought our teas too, so we could stay here a long, long time?" said Milly-Molly-Mandy.

"Umm," said Billy Blunt. "We ought to

have done. Expect we'll have to be getting back soon."

So at last as they got hungry, and thirsty too (having finished all the bottle of water), they began to pack up their things and Billy Blunt put on his socks and boots. And they tramped all the way back, scrambling up and down the banks, and jumping the stepping-stones.

When they got near home Milly-Molly-Mandy said doubtfully, "What about our fishes?"

And Billy Blunt said, "We don't really want 'em now, do we? We only wanted a fishing expedition."

So they counted how many there were (there were fifteen), and then emptied them back into the brook, where they darted off at once to their meals.

And Milly-Molly-Mandy and Billy Blunt went on up through the meadow to the nice white cottage with the thatched roof, feeling very hungry, and hoping they weren't too badly late for tea.

And when they got in Father and Mother and Grandpa and Grandma and Uncle and Aunty were all sitting at table, just finishing – what do you think?

Why, their midday dinner!

Milly-Molly-Mandy and Billy Blunt couldn't think how it had happened. But when you get up so very early to go on fishing expeditions, and get so very hungry, well, it is rather difficult to reckon the time properly!

Milly-Molly-Mandy Rides a Horse

Once upon a time Milly-Molly-Mandy was out playing at horses with little-friend-Susan and Billy Blunt.

There was a clearing in the woods near the nice white cottage with the thatched roof, where Milly-Molly-Mandy lived, and they had found some fallen branches and were galloping astride them along a mossy track.

Then Billy Blunt saw a low-growing branch of a tree which he climbed on, and sat bouncing up and down exactly like real horse-riding. Milly-Molly-Mandy and little-friend-Susan had to stop and watch him, till he let them each have a go.

Then he said firmly, "Now it's my turn." And he got on again and bounced solemnly up and down, while Milly-Molly-Mandy and little-friend-Susan pranced around on their sticks.

(Horse-riding is very good exercise!)

Presently what did they hear but a thud-thudding sound, like real horses' hoofs. And what did they see but five or six real horse-riders come riding along down the mossy track.

"Oh, look!" cried Milly-Molly-Mandy.

"Live horses!" cried little-friend-Susan.

"Mind yourselves!" called Billy Blunt, from his tree.

So they stopped well to one side as the horses passed in single file, hoofs thudding, harnesses creaking, breaths snorting.

Milly-Molly-Mandy and little-friend-Susan and Billy Blunt hardly looked at the riders till one small one in fawn knee-breeches turned her head and said, "Hullo!" to them.

It was the little girl Jessamine, who lived at the Big House with the iron railings near the cross-roads.

"Well!" said Milly-Molly-Mandy, as the party cantered out into the road towards the village, "fancy Jessamine having a real horse!"

"Isn't she lucky!" said little-friend-Susan.

"It's the riding school," said Billy Blunt. "She's learning riding."

Somehow, their pretend-horses didn't seem quite such fun now. Billy Blunt stopped bouncing and climbed down.

"I wish we'd got real horses to ride on," said Milly-Molly-Mandy.

"So do I," said little-friend-Susan.

Billy Blunt said, "Well, what about your old Twinkletoes?"

"He's Grandpa's pony," said Milly-Molly-Mandy. "He isn't meant for riding."

"He pulls their market-cart," said little-friend-Susan.

"But he is a horse," said Billy Blunt.

Milly-Molly-Mandy stood and thought.

"I don't believe they'd let us ride him," she said; "but we could *ask*, couldn't we?"

"Oh, *do*!" said little-friend-Susan.

"No harm asking," said Billy Blunt.

So they all ran down the road to the

"Oh, look!" cried Milly-Molly-Mandy

nice white cottage with the thatched roof, into the kitchen, where Mother was busy ironing shirts.

"Oh, Mother!" asked Milly-Molly-Mandy. "Please may we go horse-riding on Twinkletoes?"

"Well, now," said Mother, "you'd better see what Father has to say!"

So they ran outside to the barn, where Father was busy sorting potatoes.

"Father!" asked Milly-Molly-Mandy. "Please may we go horse-riding on Twinkletoes?"

"Why, where do you want to go?" asked Father. "Land's End or John o' Groats?"

"Oh, no," said Milly-Molly-Mandy (she wasn't sure where either of those places were), "only just in the meadow, perhaps."

"Well, now," said Father, "perhaps you'd better see what Grandpa has to say!"

So they ran around to the stable, where Grandpa was busy mending a broken strap.

"Grandpa!" asked Milly-Molly-Mandy. "Please may we go horse-riding on Twinkletoes?"

Grandpa didn't answer at once. Then he said slowly: "Well, you know, he's not exactly used to folks sitting on him, is old Twinkletoes. But we might try!"

So Grandpa tried putting a bridle on Twinkletoes and strapping an old blanket across his back for a saddle. Then he stooped to lift Milly-Molly-Mandy up.

But Milly-Molly-Mandy said quickly, "Billy Blunt ought to have first go!" (Maybe she wanted to see if Twinkletoes would mind being ridden!)

So Grandpa held the bridle while Billy Blunt got on. And after a moment Twinkletoes clip-clopped slowly across the yard with Billy Blunt sitting joggling on his back.

They all went into the meadow, and Grandpa stood by the gate, watching. It was very exciting!

"Does it feel nice?" Milly-Molly-Mandy called up to Billy Blunt.

"It looks lovely!" called little-friend-Susan.

"Not bad," returned Billy Blunt. (He was really enjoying it like anything!) "Look out you don't get under his feet!"

They went right across the meadow, and Twinkletoes didn't seem to mind a bit. When they got back to the gate again Billy Blunt slid down, and then Grandpa helped little-friend-Susan up. (Milly-Molly-Mandy had to keep jumping because it was so exciting and so hard to wait her turn! – but of course visitors should have first go.)

Little-friend-Susan only wished that old Twinkletoes wouldn't keep stopping to nibble the grass!

At last Milly-Molly-Mandy's turn came.

She was lifted on to the pony's broad back (it felt awfully high)! and off he went, with Milly-Molly-Mandy holding tight to his mane.

It was terribly thrilling! But soon she was able to sit up and look about a bit. It felt rather like being on a rocking-chair, as Twinkletoes ambled slowly along with his head drooping, while little-friend-Susan picked daisies and Billy Blunt romped with Toby the dog.

Suddenly – what *do* you think? – Twinkletoes seemed to stumble on a rough bit of ground and next moment Milly-Molly-Mandy slid sprawling over his head down into the long grass!

The others all came running to help her up, Toby the dog barking at poor Twinkletoes, who stood shaking his head in a puzzled sort of way.

"You let his head hang down, didn't you?" said Grandpa; "and he kind of went to sleep! You want to let him feel the reins, only don't pull on them. You'll learn. Up with you, now!"

But Milly-Molly-Mandy wasn't sure she wanted any more riding just at present. "It's Billy's turn again," she said.

But Billy said, "No! You should always get on at once if you fall off a horse. Go on, get on."

So then Milly-Molly-Mandy got on. And Twinkletoes trotted with her so nicely round the meadow that they all forgot about the tumble.

"Can we have some more rides soon?" asked Milly-Molly-Mandy as she got down and they all stood patting Twinkletoes.

Grandpa said, Yes, another day, when he had time to see about some stirrups.

Milly-Molly-Mandy and Billy Blunt and little-friend-Susan were glad to think they had a real horse to ride on now, like the little girl Jessamine!

Milly-Molly-Mandy Minds a Baby

Once upon a time Milly-Molly-Mandy had to mind a tiny little baby.

It was the funniest tiny little baby you could possibly imagine, and Milly-Molly-Mandy had to mind it because there didn't seem to be anybody else to do so. She couldn't find its mother or its father or any of its relations, so she had to take it home and look after it herself (because, of course, you can't leave a tiny little baby alone in a wood, with no one anywhere about to look after it).

And this is how it happened.

Milly-Molly-Mandy wanted some acorn cups (which are useful for making dolls' bowls, and wheels for matchbox carts, and all that sort of thing, you know). So, as little-friend-Susan was busy looking after her baby sister, Milly-Molly-Mandy went off to the woods with just Toby the dog to look for some.

While she was busy looking she heard a loud chirping noise. And Milly-Molly-Mandy said to herself, "I wonder what sort of bird that is?" And then she found a ripe blackberry, and forgot about the chirping noise.

After a time Milly-Molly-Mandy said to herself, "How that bird does keep on chirping!" And then Toby the dog found a rabbit hole, and Milly-Molly-Mandy forgot again about the chirping noise.

After some more time Milly-Molly-Mandy said to herself, "That bird sounds as

if it wants something." And then Milly-Molly-Mandy went towards a brambly clearing in the wood from which the chirping noise seemed to come.

But when she got there the chirping noise didn't seem to come from a tree, but from a low bramble bush. And when she got to the low bramble bush the chirping noise stopped.

Milly-Molly-Mandy thought that was because it was frightened of her. So she said out loud, "It's all right – don't be frightened. It's only me!" just as kindly as she could, and then she poked about in among the bramble bush. But she couldn't find anything, except thorns.

And then, quite suddenly, lying in the

grass on the other side of the bramble bush, Milly-Molly-Mandy and Toby the dog together found what had been making all the chirping noise. It was so frightened that it had rolled itself into a tight little prickly ball, no bigger than the penny india rubber ball which Milly-Molly-Mandy had bought at Miss Muggins's shop the day before.

For what DO you think it was? A little tiny weeny baby hedgehog!

Milly-Molly-Mandy was excited! And so was Toby the dog! Milly-Molly-Mandy had to say, "No, Toby! Be quiet, Toby!" very firmly indeed. And then she picked up the baby hedgehog in a bracken leaf (because it was a very prickly baby, though it was so small), and she could just see its little soft nose quivering among its prickles.

Then Milly-Molly-Mandy looked about to find its nest (for, of course, she didn't want to take it away from its family), but she couldn't find it. And then the baby began squeaking again for its mother, but its mother didn't come.

So at last Milly-Molly-Mandy said comfortingly, "Never mind, darling – I'll take you home and look after you!"

So Milly-Molly-Mandy carried the baby hedgehog between her two hands very carefully; and it unrolled itself a bit and quivered its little soft nose over her fingers as if it hoped they might be good to eat, and it squeaked and squeaked, because it was very hungry. So Milly-Molly-Mandy hurried all she could, and Toby the dog capered along at her side, and at last they got home to the nice white cottage with the thatched roof.

Father and Mother and Grandpa and Grandma and Uncle and Aunty were all very interested indeed.

Mother put a saucer of milk on the stove to warm, and then they tried to feed the baby. But it was too little to lap from a saucer, and it was too little even to lick from Milly-Molly-Mandy's finger. So at last they had to wait until it opened its mouth to squeak and then squirt drops of warm milk into it with Father's fountain pen filler!

After that the baby felt a bit happier, and Milly-Molly-Mandy made it a nest in a little box of hay. But when she put it in it squeaked and squeaked again for its nice warm mother till Milly-Molly-Mandy put

They were all very interested indeed

her hand in the box; and then it snuggled up against it and went to sleep. And Milly-Molly-Mandy stood there and chuckled softly to herself, because it felt so funny being mistaken for Mrs Hedgehog! (She quite liked it!)

When Father and Grandpa and Uncle came in to dinner the baby woke and began squeaking again. So Uncle picked it up in his big hand to have a look at it, while Milly-Molly-Mandy ran for more milk and the fountain pen filler.

And the baby squeaked so loudly that Uncle said, "Hul-lo, Horace! What's all this noise about!" And Milly-Molly-Mandy was pleased, because "Horace" just seemed to suit the baby hedgehog, and no one knew what its mother had named it (but I don't suppose it was Horace!).

Milly-Molly-Mandy was kept very busy all that day feeding Horace every hour or two. He was so prickly that she had to wrap him round in an old handkerchief first – and he looked the funniest little baby in a white shawl you ever did see!

When bedtime came Milly-Molly-Mandy wanted to take the hedgehog's box up to her little room with her. But Mother said no, he would be all right in the kitchen till morning. So they gave him a hot bottle to snuggle against (it was an ink bottle, wrapped in flannel), and then Milly-Molly-Mandy went off to bed.

But being "mother" even to a hedgehog is very important sort of job, and in the night Milly-Molly-Mandy woke up and thought of Horace, and wondered if he felt lonely in his new home.

And she creepy-crept in the dark to the top of the stairs and listened.

And after a time she heard a tiny little

"Squeak! Squeak!" coming from the kitchen. So she hurried and pulled on her dressing-gown and her bedroom slippers, and then she hurried and creepy-crept in the dark downstairs into the kitchen, and carefully lit the candle on the dresser.

And then she fed Horace and talked to him in a comfortable whisper, so that he didn't feel lonely any more. And then she put him back to bed and blew out the candle, and creepy-crept in the dark upstairs to her own little bed. (And it did feel so nice and warm to get into again!)

Next day Horace learned to open his mouth when he felt the fountain pen filler touch it (he couldn't see, because his eyes weren't open yet – just like a baby puppy or kitten). And quite soon he learned to suck away at the filler just as if it were a proper baby's bottle! And he grew and he grew, and in a week's time his eyes were open. And soon he grew little teeth, and could gobble bread and milk out of an egg-cup, and sometimes a little bit of meat or banana.

He was quite a little-boy hedgehog now, instead of a little baby one, and Milly-Molly-Mandy didn't need to get up in the night any more to feed him.

Milly-Molly-Mandy was very proud of him, and when little-friend-Susan used to say she had to hurry home after school to look after her baby sister, Milly-Molly-Mandy used to say she had to hurry too to look after the baby Horace. She used to give him walks in the garden, and laugh at his funny little back legs and tiny tail as he waddled about, nosing the ground. When

Toby the dog barked he would roll himself up into a prickly ball in a second; but he soon came out again, and would run to Milly-Molly-Mandy's hand when she called "Horace!" (He was quite happy with her for a mother.)

One day Horace got out of his hay-box in the kitchen, and they couldn't find him for a long time, though they all looked – Father and Mother and Grandpa and Grandma and Uncle and Aunty and Milly-Molly-Mandy. But at last where do you think they found him? – in the larder!

"Well!" said Uncle, "Horace knows how to look after himself all right now!"

After that Horace's bed was put out in the barn, and Milly-Molly-Mandy would take his little basin of bread and milk out to him, and stay and play till it got too chilly.

And then, one frosty morning, they couldn't find Horace anywhere, though they all looked – Father and Mother and Grandpa and Grandma and Uncle and Aunty and Milly-Molly-Mandy. But at last, a day or two after, Grandpa was pulling out some hay for the pony Twinkletoes, when what do you think he found! A little ball of prickles cuddled up deep in the hay!

Horace had gone to sleep for the winter, like the proper little hedgehog he was! (Grandpa said that sort of going to sleep was called "hibernating".)

So Milly-Molly-Mandy put the hay with the prickly ball inside it into a large box in the barn, with a little bowl of water near by (in case Horace should wake up and want a drink).

And there she left him (sleeping soundly while the cold winds blew and the snows fell) until he should wake up in the spring and come out to play with her again!

(And that's a true story!)

Joyce Lankester Brisley

MILLY-MOLLY-MANDY'S Family

Once upon a time there was a little girl. She had a Father, and a Mother, and a Grandpa, and a Grandma, and an Uncle, and an Aunty; and they all lived together in a nice white cottage with a thatched roof.

Milly-Molly-Mandy has a very big family and she loves them all very much. Join her as she organizes a party for her grandparents and a surprise for her mother, runs errands for the whole family and steals the show at the village concert!

Joyce Lankester Brisley

MILLY-MOLLY-MANDY'S Friends

"Let's both dress up and be ladies," said Milly-Molly-Mandy. "Ooh, yes, let's," said little-friend-Susan.

Milly-Molly-Mandy has lots of friends, but her favourite companions are little-friend-Susan and Billy Blunt. Join them on five of their exciting adventures as they run races, pay visits, rescue rabbits, play tricks on one another and deal with a gang of naughty boys!

Joyce Lankester Brisley

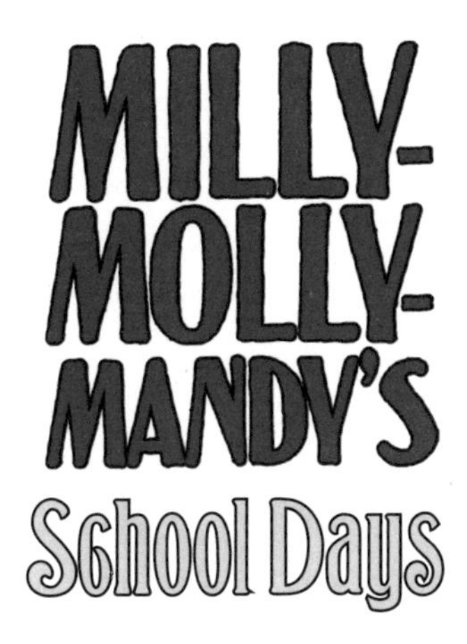

On Monday Milly-Molly-Mandy was in a great hurry to finish her breakfast and be off very early to school.

Milly-Molly-Mandy always has fun at school – join her as she gets to know her teacher, makes a feathery friend and learns lots of exciting things. Even getting to school can be an adventure when it's raining or snowing, but Milly-Molly-Mandy always gets there in the end!

MILLY-MOLLY-MANDY'S Things to Make and Do

Based on the stories by

JOYCE LANKESTER BRISLEY

Whether she's baking a cake, planting a miniature garden or having a dolls' tea-party, Milly-Molly-Mandy is always having fun. Packed with teatime treats, crafty fun and big ideas to brighten up a gloomy day, this is the perfect book for long holidays, rainy days and adventures in your own back garden!

With easy-to-follow instructions for lots of wonderful activities, including:

- ❖ Baking blackberry crumble
- ❖ Sewing patchwork
- ❖ Knitting a scarf
- ❖ Planting sunflowers
- ❖ Identifying leaves
- ❖ Building a fort
- ❖ Making a bird feeder

And much, much more!

A selected list of titles available from Macmillan Children's Books

The prices shown below are correct at the time of going to press. However, Macmillan Publishers reserves the right to show new retail prices on covers, which may differ from those previously advertised.

Joyce Lankester Brisley

Milly-Molly-Mandy's Family	978-0-230-75498-0	£5.99
Milly-Molly-Mandy's Friends	978-0-230-75497-3	£5.99
Milly-Molly-Mandy's School Days	978-0-230-75502-4	£5.99
Milly-Molly-Mandy's Things to Make and Do	978-0-230-75494-2	£12.99
The Milly-Molly-Mandy Storybook	978-0-230-74407-3	£9.99
More Milly-Molly-Mandy	978-0-230-74381-6	£9.99

All Pan Macmillan titles can be ordered from our website, www.panmacmillan.com, or from your local bookshop and are also available by post from:

Bookpost, PO Box 29, Douglas, Isle of Man IM99 1BQ

Credit cards accepted. For details:

Telephone: 01624 677237

Fax: 01624 670923

Email: bookshop@enterprise.net

www.bookpost.co.uk

Free postage and packing in the United Kingdom

The Nice White Cottage with the Thatched Roof (where Milly-Molly-Mandy lives)
Brook
The Meadow (where M-M-M and Billy Blunt practised racing)
The Barn (where M-M-M gave a party)
The Moggs's Cottage (where little-friend-Susan lives)
Short cut to School (only used in dry weather)
Woods
To Another Village
MAP of